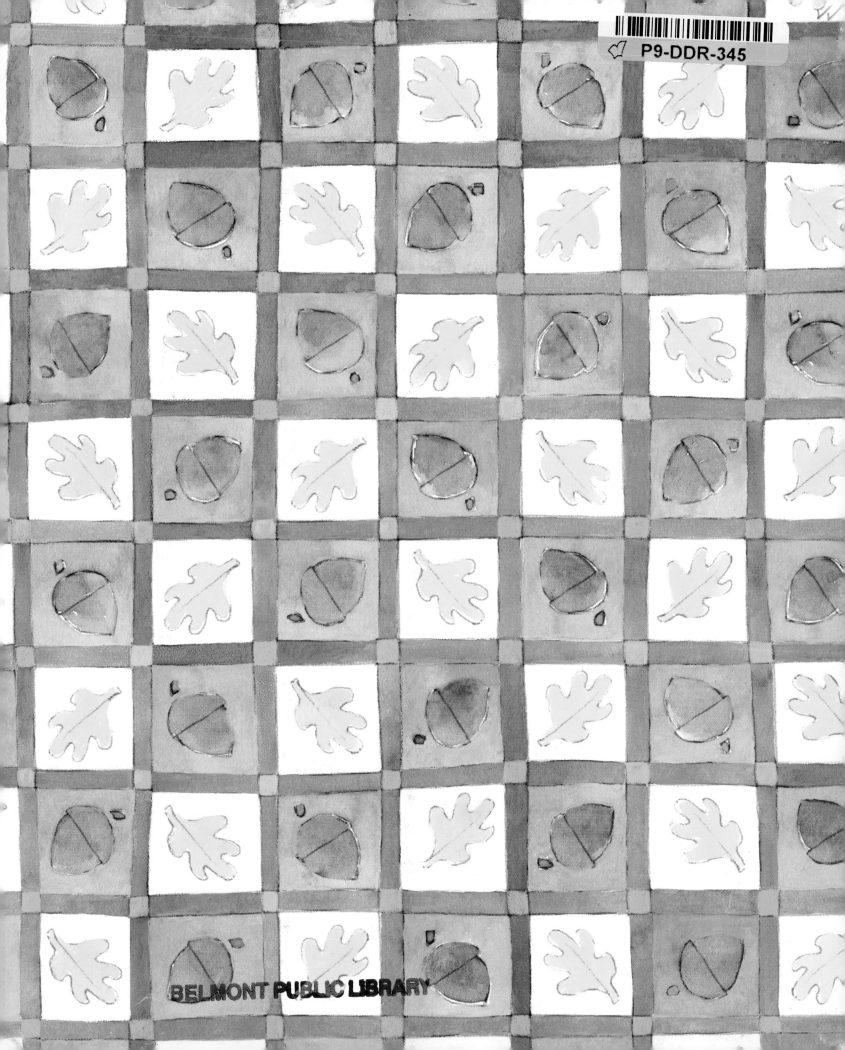

For my nutty and talented group of author friends—
Hope Vestergaard, Lisa Wheeler, Kelly DiPucchio,
Paula Yoo, Carolyn Crimi, and April Young Fritz.
My deepest gratitude,
J. B.

Copyright © 2006 by Janie Bynum

First edition 2006

Library of Congress Cataloging-in-Publication Data

Bynum, Janie.
Nutmeg and Barley: a budding friendship / Janie Bynum.—1st ed.
p. cm.
Summary: Neighbors Nutmeg the squirrel and Barley the mouse
believe that they have nothing in common until an emergency
forces them to discover surprising things about each other.
ISBN 0-7636-2382-2
[1. Squirrels—Fiction. 2. Mice—Fiction.
3. Neighborliness—Fiction. I. Title.
PZ7.B97Nu 2005
[E]—dc22 2004065015

2 4 6 8 10 9 7 5 3 1

Printed in China

This book was typeset in Colwell.
The illustrations were done in watercolor, pencil, and pastel.

Candlewick Press
2067 Massachusetts Avenue
Cambridge, Massachusetts 02140

visit us at www.candlewick.com

NUTMEG AND BARLEY

A BUDDING FRIENDSHIP

Janie Bynum

CANDLEWICK PRESS
CAMBRIDGE, MASSACHUSETTS

In Moosejaw County, on the edge of the woods, lived two neighbors—who had nothing in common.

Halfway up an old pecan tree lived a chatty red squirrel. Nutmeg loved bright sunshine and loud thunderstorms. But most of all, she loved to dance to her favorite forest tune.

In a hollow log below, a quiet gray mouse made his home. Barley loved cool shade and gentle breezes. And at the end of the day, he loved to relax with a little music.

Every morning, Nutmeg chattered in the branches with the other squirrels while Barley played a game of solitaire.

"Hey, neighbor!" Nutmeg often called. "Why don't you join us for a little gossip?"

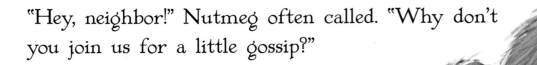

"No, thanks. I'm busy," Barley always replied.

Every afternoon, Barley tended his garden while Nutmeg soaked up the sunshine. Every afternoon, Nutmeg called to her neighbor, "Come on up for a visit. The view is delicious!"

As usual, Barley just shook his head and went back to weeding, stopping only for a cup of tea—which he sipped alone.

Never before had Nutmeg known a
rodent she couldn't charm.

"I don't suppose we have a thing in
common anyway," Nutmeg said
before she turned away.

But later, Nutmeg found fresh flowers on her doorstep.
And she knew exactly who had left them there.

The next day, Nutmeg went to thank Barley for the gift. As she got close to Barley's house, a squeaky groan drifted out through the window.

"Barley, are you okay?" she called out. "Do you need anything?"

Barley sneezed. "Would love some tea!"

But through a whistling wind, Nutmeg heard, "Should leave me be!"

So Nutmeg left.

Night fell and Nutmeg needed cheering up.
Maybe dancing would make her feel better.

"Hey, someone start the music," she called.
But all she heard was the soft rustle of leaves.

Days went by, and Nutmeg hadn't
seen Barley even once. But she was
determined not to worry about the
rude little rodent.

Nutmeg opened a book and
tried to read. But she
couldn't sit still.

She made her favorite snack—pecan biscuits with
tickleberry tea. But she wasn't hungry.

Finally Nutmeg decided that flowers might brighten her mood.
And she knew just where to go for the freshest ones.

Nutmeg went and tapped on Barley's door.
No one answered. When she knocked a
little harder, the door flew open.

There lay Barley, shivering under a
threadbare blanket.

"Oh, Barley," cried Nutmeg,
"chills in the middle of summer?
You must have an awful fever."

Barley tried to sit up.
"I was hoping you'd come back,"
he moaned.

"Lie down," Nutmeg ordered.
"I'll just be a moment."

Nutmeg hurried home and soon returned with piles of blankets and plenty of food.

She built a fire in the old wood stove and brewed some tea for her sick little neighbor.

She read her favorite books to Barley. She sat up with him all night, making sure he was extra comfortable.

By daybreak, Nutmeg looked quite comfortable, too.
And Barley felt much better.

That morning, Nutmeg awoke to a familiar melody.

She flew outside to investigate.

"BARLEY! It's YOU!
You're the one who makes my favorite dancing music!"

"Yes," her new friend replied.
"And now it's time we dance!"

In Moosejaw County, on the edge of the woods, live two neighbors who now have a couple of things in common— a love for lively music and their heartfelt friendship.

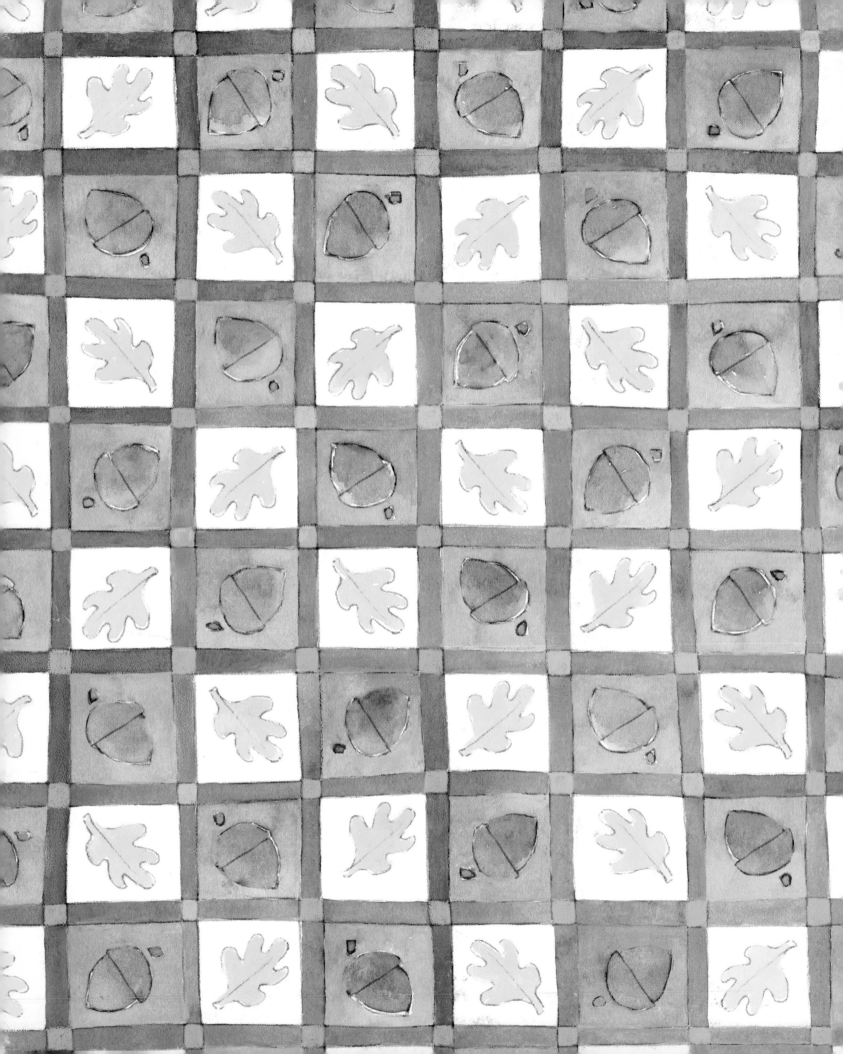